# Something

# Special

By the same author

FICTION

*Under the Net*
*The Flight from the Enchanter*
*The Sandcastle*
*The Bell*
*A Severed Head*
*An Unofficial Rose*
*The Unicorn*
*The Italian Girl*
*The Red and the Green*
*The Time of the Angels*
*The Nice and the Good*
*Bruno's Dream*
*A Fairly Honourable Defeat*
*An Accidental Man*
*The Black Prince*
*The Sacred and Profane Love Machine*
*A World Child*
*Henry and Cato*
*The Sea, the Sea*
*Nuns and Soldiers*
*The Philosopher's Pupil*
*The Good Apprentice*
*The Book and the Brotherhood*
*The Message to the Planet*
*The Green Knight*
*Jackson's Dilemma*
*Something Special*

PHILOSOPHY

*Sartre, Romantic Rationalist*
*Metaphysics as a Guide to Morals*
*Existentialists and Mystics*

POETRY

*A Year of Birds*

# SOMETHING SPECIAL

## A STORY

*Iris Murdoch*

*Illustrated by Michael McCurdy*

W. W. Norton & Company
New York • London

This story was first published in *Winter's Tales No. 3* in 1957. It was also published in 1959 in Japan in an English language textbook with Japanese annotations.

This edition first published in the United States in 2000 by W. W. Norton & Company.


Printed in Mexico

The text and display of this book are composed in Fournier
Composition by Allentown Digital Services
Division of R.R. Donnelley & Sons Company
Manufactured in Mexico
Book design by Dana Sloan

Library of Congress Cataloging-in-Publication Data

Murdoch, Iris.
Something special : a story / Iris Murdoch ; illustrated by Michael McCurdy.
p. cm.
ISBN 0-393-05007-6
1. Dublin (Ireland)—Fiction. 2. Young women—Fiction.
I. McCurdy, Michael. II. Title.
PR6063.U7 S66 2000
823'.914—dc21
00-040212

W. W. Norton & Company, Inc., 500 Fifth Avenue, New York, N.Y. 10110
www.wwnorton.com

W. W. Norton & Company Ltd., 10 Coptic Street, London WC1A 1PU

1 2 3 4 5 6 7 8 9 0

# Contents

# Something

# Special

"Why wouldn't you take him now?" said Mrs Geary. She was setting the evening papers to rights on the counter.

Yvonne sat astride a chair in the middle of the shop. She had it tilting precariously and was rubbing her small head animal fashion on the wood of the back, while her long legs were braced to prevent herself from toppling over. In answer to the question she said nothing.

"She's cross again," said her uncle, who was standing at the door of the inner room.

"Who's she? She's the cat!" said Yvonne. She began to rock the chair violently to and fro.

"Don't be breaking down that chair," said her mother. "It's the last we have of the decent ones till the cane man is back. Why wouldn't you take him is what I asked."

Close outside the shop the tram for Dublin came rattling by, darkening the scene for a moment and making little objects on the higher shelves jump and tinkle. It was a hot evening and the doors stood wide open to the dust of the street.

"Oh leave off, leave off!" said Yvonne. "I don't *want* him, I don't *want* to marry. He's nothing special."

"Nothing special is it?" said her uncle. "He's a nice young man in a steady job and he wants to wed you and you no longer so young. Or would you be living all your life on your ma?"

"If you won't wed him you shouldn't be leading him up the garden," said her mother, "and leave breaking that chair."

"Can't I be ordinary friends with a boy," said Yvonne, "without the pair of you being at me? I'm twenty-four and I know what I'm about."

"You're twenty-four indeed," said her mother, "and there's Betty Nolan and Maureen Burke are married these three years and they in a lower form than you at school."

"I'm not the like of those two," said Yvonne.

"True for you!" said her mother.

"It's the women's magazines," said her uncle, "and the little novels she's for ever reading that are putting ideas in her head until she won't marry except it's the Sheik of Araby."

"It's little enough she finds to do with her time," said her mother, "so that she's always in there in the little dark room, flat on her tum with her nose inside a novel till it's a wonder her two eyes aren't worn away in her head."

"Can't I live my life as I please," said Yvonne, "since it's the only thing I have? It's that I can't see him as something special and I won't marry him if I can't."

"He's one of the Chosen People," said her uncle. "Isn't that special enough?"

"Don't start on that thing again," said her

mother. "Sam's a nice young fellow, and not like the run of the Jew-boys at all. He'd bring the children up Church of Ireland."

"At that," said her uncle, "it's better than the other lot with the little priest after them the whole time and bobbing their hats at the chapel doors so you can't even have a peaceful ride on the tram. I've nothing against the Jews."

"Our Lord was a Jew," said Yvonne.

"Don't be saying bold things like that!" said her mother.

"Our Lord was the Son of God," said her uncle, "and that's neither Jew nor Greek."

"Is it this evening the Christmas card man is coming?" said Yvonne.

"It is," said her mother, "though why they want to be bothering us with Christmas cards in the middle of summer I'm at a loss to know."

"I'll wait by and see him," said Yvonne. "You always pick the dull ones."

"I pick the ones that sell," said her mother, "and don't you be after hanging around acting the maggot when Sam comes, there's little enough room in there."

"If you were married at least you'd be out of this," said her uncle, "and it isn't your ma you'd be sharing a bed with then, and you always complaining about the poky hole this place is."

"It is a poky hole," said Yvonne, "but then I'd be in another poky hole some other place."

"I'm tired telling you," said her mother, "you could get one of those new little houses off the Drumcondra Road. The man in Macmullan's shop knows the man that keeps the list."

"I don't want a new little house," said Yvonne. "I tell you I don't see him right and that's that!"

"If you wait till you marry for love," said her uncle, "you'll wait ten years and then make a foolish match. You're not Greta Garbo and you're lucky there's a young fellow after you at all. Sensible people marry because they want to be in the married state and not because of feelings they have in their breasts."

"She's still stuck on the English lad," said her

mother, "the tall fellow, Tony Thingummy was his name."

"I am not!" said Yvonne. "Good riddance to bad rubbish!"

"I could not abide his voice," said her uncle. "He had his mouth all prissed up when he talked, like a man was acting in a play."

"Isn't it the like of the bloody English to win the Sweep again this year?" said her mother.

"He brought me flowers," said Yvonne.

"Flowers is it!" said her uncle. "And singing little songs to you you said once!"

"He was a jaunty boy," said her mother, "and a fine slim thing with some pretty ways to him, but he's gone now. And you wait till you see what Sam'll bring you one of these days."

"Ah, you're potty with that diamond ring story," said her uncle. "You'll turn the child's head on her. That fellow's as poor as we are."

"There's nobody is as poor as we are," said Yvonne.

"He's a hired man," said her uncle. "I don't deny he may get to have his own tailoring shop one day and be his own master. I can see that in him, that he's not a Jew for nothing. But he's no fancy worker now and he's poorly off."

"Those ones are never poor," said her mother. "They just pretend to be so their own people won't be taking their bits of money off them."

"It's near his time to come," said Yvonne. "Don't be talking about him when he comes in, it's not manners."

"Listen who's mentioning manners!" said her uncle.

"You recall the time," said her mother, "we met him at poor Mr Stacey's sale and we went to Sullavan's bar after and he paid for two rounds?"

"He was for catching Yvonne's eye," said her uncle, "with flashing his wad around. I'll lay he had to walk home."

"You're a fine one," said her mother, "and you telling me to encourage the child!"

"Did I ever say she should marry him for his money?" said her uncle.

"Well, you'll see," said her mother. "It's the custom of those ones. When they want to be engaged to a girl they suddenly bring the diamond ring out and the girl says yes."

"If they do it's on hire from the pop shop," said her uncle, "and it's back in the window directly."

"What's Julia Batey's ring then?" said her mother, "and what's her name, young Polly's sister, who married Jews the pair of them, and it happened that way with both. One evening quite suddenly 'I want to show you something' says he, and there was the ring and they were engaged from then. I tell you it's a custom."

"Well, I hope you're right I'm sure," said her uncle. "It might be just the thing that would make up the grand young lady's mind. A diamond ring now, that would be something special, wouldn't it?"

"A diamond ring," said Yvonne, "would be a change at least."

"Perhaps he'll have it with him this very night!" said her mother.

"I *don't* think!" said Yvonne.

"Where are you off to anyway?" said her mother.

"I haven't the faintest," said Yvonne. "Into town, I suppose."

"You might go down the pier," said her uncle, "and see the mail boat out. That would be better for you than sitting in those stuffy bars or walking along the Liffey breathing the foul airs of the river, and coming home smelling of Guinness."

"Besides, you know Sam likes the sea," said her mother. "He's been all day long dying of suffocation in that steamy room with the clothes press."

"It's more fun in town," said Yvonne. "They've the decorations up for Ireland At Home. And I've been all day long dying of boredom in Kingstown."

"It's well for you," said her uncle, "that it's Sam that pays!"

"And I don't like your going into those low places," said her mother. "That's not Sam's idea, I know, it's you. Sam's not a one for sitting dreaming in a bar. That's another thing I like about him."

"Kimball's have got a new saloon lounge," said Yvonne, "like a real drawing-room done up with flowers and those crystal lights. Maybe we'll go there."

"You'll pay extra!" said her uncle.

"Let Sam worry about that!" said her mother. "It's a relief they have those saloon lounges in the pubs nowadays where you can get away from the smell of porter and a lady can sit there without being taken for something else."

"Here's the Christmas card man!" said Yvonne, and jumped up from her chair.

"Why, Mr Lynch," said Mrs Geary, "it's a pleasure to see you again, who'd think a whole year had gone by, it seems like yesterday you were here before."

"Good evening, Mrs Geary," said Mr Lynch,

"it's a blessing to see you looking so well, and Miss Geary and Mr O'Brien still with you. Change and decay in all around we see. I'm told poor Mrs Taylor at the place in Monkstown has passed on since now a year ago."

"Yes, the poor old faggot," said Mrs Geary, "but after seventy years you can't complain, can you? The good Lord's lending it to you after that."

"Our time is always on loan, Mrs Geary," said Mr Lynch, "and who knows when the great Creditor will call? We are as grass which to-day flourisheth and to-morrow it is cast into the oven."

"We'll go through," said Mrs Geary, "and Mr O'Brien will mind the shop."

Yvonne and her mother went into the inner room, followed by Mr Lynch. The inner room was very dark, lit only on the far side by a window of frosted glass that gave onto the kitchen. It had a bedroom smell of ancient fabrics and perspiration and dust. Mrs Geary turned on the light. The mountainous double bed with its great white

quilt and brass knobs and rails, wherein she and her daughter slept, took up half the room. A shiny horsehair sofa took up most of the other half, leaving space for a small velvet-topped table and three black chairs which stood in a row in front of the towering mantelshelf where photographs and brass animals rose in tiers to the ceiling. Mr Lynch opened his suitcase and began to spread out the Christmas cards on the faded red velvet.

"The robin and the snow go well," said Mrs Geary, "and the stage-coach is popular and the church lit up at night."

"The traditional themes of Christmas-tide," said Mr Lynch, "have a universal appeal."

"Oh look," said Yvonne, "that's the nicest one I've *ever* seen! Now that's really special." She held it aloft. A frame of glossy golden cardboard enclosed a little square of white silk on which some roses were embroidered.

"That's a novelty," said Mr Lynch, "and comes a bit more expensive."

"It's not like a true Christmas card, the fancy thing," said Mrs Geary. "I always think a nice picture and a nice verse is what you want. The sentiment is all."

"Here's Sam," said Mr O'Brien from the shop.

Sam came and stood in the doorway from the shop, frowning in the electric light. He was a short man, "portly" Mr O'Brien called him, and he could hardly count as handsome. He had a pale moon-face and fugitive hands, but his eyes were dark, and his dark bushy head of hair was like the brave plume of a bird. He had his best suit on, which was a midnight blue with a grey stripe, and his tie was of light yellow silk.

"Come on in, Sam," said Mrs Geary. "Yvonne's been ready this long time. Mr Lynch, this is Mr Goldman."

"How do you do?" they said.

"You're mighty smart to-night, Sam," said Mrs Geary. "Going to have a special evening?"

"We're choosing the Christmas cards," said Yvonne. "Have you got any with the ox and the ass on, Mr Lynch?"

"Here," said Mr Lynch, "we have the ox and the ass, and here we see our Lord lying in the manger, and His Mother by, and here the three Maji with their costly gifts, and here the angels coming to the poor shepherds by night, and here the star of glory that led them on. When Jesus was born in Bethlehem of Judaea in the days of Herod the King —"

"I still like this one best," said Yvonne.

"Look, Sam, isn't that pretty?" She held up the card with the golden frame.

"You two be off now," said Mrs Geary, "and leave troubling Sam with these Christian things."

"I don't mind," said Sam. "I always observe Christmas just as you do, Mrs Geary. I take it as a sort of emblem."

"That's right," said Mr Lynch. "What after all divides us one from another? In My Father's house are many mansions. If it were not so I would have told you."

"I'll just get my coat," said Yvonne.

"Don't keep her out late, Sam," said Mrs Geary, "Good-bye now, and mind you have a really nice evening."

"Abyssinia," said Yvonne.

They left the cool musty air of the shop and emerged into the big warm perfumed summer dusk. Yvonne threw her head back, and pranced along in her high-heeled shoes, wearing the look of petulant intensity which she always affected for the benefit of Sam. She would not take his arm, and they went a little aimlessly down the street.

"Where shall we go?" said Sam.

"I don't mind," she said.

"We might walk a bit by the sea," said Sam, "and sit on the rocks beyond the Baths."

"It's too windy down there and I can't go on the rocks in these shoes."

"Well, let's go into town."

At that moment from the seaward side came a sonorous booming sound, very deep and sad. It came again, was sustained in a melancholy roar, and died slowly away.

"Ah, the mail boat!" said Sam. "Let's just see it out, it's ages since I saw it out."

They walked briskly as far as the Mariners' Church and turned along the front into the racing breeze. In the evening light the scene before them glowed like a coloured postcard. The mail boat had its lights on already, making pale, shifting reflections in the water which was still glossy with daylight. As they came nearer the boat began to move very slowly, and drew away from the big brown

wooden quay revealing upon it the rows and rows of people left behind agitating their white handkerchiefs in the darkening air. The scene was utterly silent. A curly plume of black smoke gathered upon the metallic water, hid the ship for a moment, and then lifted to show it gliding away between the two lighthouses, whose beams were kindled at that very time, and into the open sea. Beyond it a large pale moon was rising over Howth Head.

"The moon hath raised her lamp above," said Sam.

"I've seen the mail boat out a hundred times," said Yvonne, "and one day I'll be on it."

"Would you like to go to England then?" said Sam.

Yvonne gave him a look of exaggerated scorn. "Doesn't every Irish person with a soul in them want to go to England?" she said.

They walked more slowly back now, past the golden windows of Ross's Hotel to take the Dublin tram. By the time they had climbed the hill the ship was half-way toward the horizon, its trail of smoke

taken up into the gathering night, and by the time they got off the tram at Nelson's Pillar the daylight was gone entirely.

"Now where would you like to go?" said Sam.

"Don't be eternally asking me that question!" she said. "Just go somewhere yourself and I'll probably follow!"

Sam took her arm, which she let him hold this time, and walked her back toward O'Connell Bridge and along onto the quays. The Liffey flowed past them, oily and glistening, as black as Guinness, bound for Dublin Bay. It had not far to go now. Along the parapet at intervals, and hanging suspended from the iron tracery of the street lamps, were metal baskets full of flowers, while a banner hanging on the bridge announced in English and in Irish that Ireland was At Home to visitors. There was a mingled smell of garbage and pollen.

Sam turned her toward the river, and was for lingering there in a sentimental way, his arm creeping about her waist. The moon was risen now over the top of the houses. But Yvonne said firmly, "You'll get your death with the smell of the drains here. Let's go to Kimball's place and try the new saloon lounge."

They turned up the side street that led to Kimball's. It was a dirty, dark little street, but a blaze of light and a good deal of hubbub at the far end of it declared the whereabouts of that hostelry. The ordinary bar, which had formerly been the only one, was in the basement, while on the street level was Kimball's grocery store, and above this the saloon lounge before mentioned. From the well of the stairs below came an odour of men and drink and the tinkling of a piano and an uproar of male voices.

Sam and Yvonne turned aside and mounted a brightly lit carpeted stairway, which smelt strongly of new paint, and emerged into the lounge. The door shut itself quietly behind them. Here everything was still. Yvonne walked across the heavy carpet and sat down on a fat chintz sofa and arranged her dress. In the gilded mirror behind the bar she could see the reflection of Sam's face as he ordered a gin and lime for her and a draught Guinness for himself. For an instant she concentrated the glow of her imagination upon him; but could only notice that he leaned forward in an apologetic way to the barman, and how absurdly his small feet turned out as he stood there. He gave the order in a low voice, as if he were asking for something not quite nice at the chemist's. A few couples sat scattered about the room, huddled under the shaded lights, murmuring to each other.

When Sam came back with the drinks Yvonne said loudly, "You'd think you were in a church here, not in a public-house!"

"Sssh!" said Sam. One or two people stared. Sam sat down close beside her on the sofa, trying to make himself shrink. He edged nearer still, but curling into himself like a hedgehog so as to be as near as possible without giving offence. He put down his glass on the table and began laboriously in his mind the long search for words, for the simple words that would lead on to the more important ones. His pale stumpy hand caressed Yvonne's bony brown hand. Hers lay there listlessly in a way that was familiar to him. He squeezed it a little and tried to draw her back towards him, deeper into the sofa. So they sat there a while in silence, Sam searching and holding, and Yvonne stiff. The upholstered stillness around them was not good for their talk. The barman chinked a glass and everyone in the room jumped.

"This place gives me heart disease," said Yvonne. "It's like a lot of dead people giving a party. Let's go and see what it's like downstairs. I've never been downstairs here."

"It's not nice," said Sam. "Ladies don't go downstairs. Why not let's go back to Henry Street? There's the little coffee bar you liked once."

"That was a silly place!" said Yvonne. "I'm going downstairs anyway. You can do as you like." She said this in a loud voice, and then got up and walked firmly toward the door. Sam, red with embarrassment, jumped up too, took a hasty pull at his drink, and followed her out. They descended into the street and took the iron staircase that led to the basement. The noise and the smell were stronger than before.

Yvonne hesitated half-way down. "You'd better lead," she said. Sam stumbled past her and pushed at the blackened door of the bar. He had never been down those stairs either.

They came out into a very big low-roofed room with white tiled walls and blazing unshaded lights. The floor was slimy with spilt drink and beery sawdust and the atmosphere was thick. The pounding repetitive beat of a piano, its melody absorbed into the continuous din of voices, was felt rather than heard. A great many men who were adhering to a circular bar in the centre, turned to stare at Yvonne as she entered. It looked at first as if no women were present, but as the haze shifted here and there it was possible to discern one or two lurking in the darkened alcoves.

"There *are* women here!" called Yvonne triumphantly.

"Not nice ones," said Sam. "What's your drink?" He hated being looked at.

"Whisky," said Yvonne. She refused to sit down, but stood there swaying slightly and holding onto one of the ironwork pillars that circled the bar. The men near by studied her with insolent appreciation and made remarks. She coloured a little, but stared straight in front of her, bright-eyed.

It was not easy for poor Sam to get at the bar. The clients who were standing in his way were in no hurry to move, though they looked at him amiably enough. The bartender, an infernal version of his upstairs colleague, pointedly served two latercomers first, and then with ironic politeness handed Sam the drinks.

"Isn't this better than up there?" Yvonne shouted, seizing her glass from him as he got back to her side.

"That's the stuff 'll put the red neck on you!" observed a man with a penetrating voice, who was standing close to Yvonne.

"Your mother something or other," Sam shouted back, propelling Yvonne fussily into a space in the middle of the floor, where he stood holding tightly onto her arm.

She stopped trying to hear his voice and gave herself up to the pleasure of being part of such a noisy crowded drunken scene. By the time she had sipped the half of her whisky she was perceptibly enjoying herself very much indeed. Upon the confused flood of noise and movement she was now afloat.

After a short while there was something quite particular to watch: a little scene which seemed to be developing on the near side of the bar.

Someone was waving his arms and shouting in an angry voice. Whereon the publican in even higher tones was heard to cry, "Just raise your hand again, mister, and you're out in the street! Patsy, put that gentleman out in the street!"

People crowded quickly forward from the alcoves to see the fun. The piano stopped abruptly and the sound of voices became suddenly jagged and harsh. A woman with a red carnation in her hair and an overwhelming perfume came and stood beside Yvonne, her bare arm touching the girl's sleeve. Yvonne could see at once that she was not a nice sort of woman at all, and she removed herself from the contact. The woman gave her a provoking stare.

"Time for us to make tracks," said Sam to Yvonne.

"Ah shut up!" she said, looking past him with glowing eyes to where the drama was unfolding.

A tall thin young fellow, the prey designate of Patsy, was swaying to and fro, still flourishing his fist, and trying to make a statement, intended no doubt as insult or vindication, but whose complexity was such that he began it several times over without succeeding in making himself clear. His antagonist, a thick man with a Cork accent, who accompanied these attempts with a continual sneering noise, suddenly gave him a violent jab in the stomach. The young man oscillated, and lurched back amid laughter, with a look of extreme surprise. To keep his balance he twisted dexterously about on his heel and found himself face to face with Yvonne.

"Ah!" said the young man. He stood there poised, frozen in the gesture of turning, with one hand outstretched ballet-wise, and slowly allowed a look of imbecile delight to transfigure his features. Another laugh went up.

"Ah!" said the young man. "I thought the flowers were all falling, but here is a rose in the bud!" He seemed to have found his tongue.

The woman with the red carnation clapped Yvonne on the shoulder. "Come along the little pet," she cried, "and give the kind gentleman a good answer!"

The thin young man turned upon her. "You

leave the young lady alone," he shouted, "she isn't your like!" And with that he darted out his hand and plucked the red carnation from the woman's hair and thrust it with another lurch into the bosom of Yvonne's frock. There was a roar of applause.

Yvonne sprang away. The woman turned quick as a flash and slapped the young man in the face. But quicker still the woman's escort, a brown man with an arm like an ape, had snatched the flower back from where it hung at Yvonne's breast and given her a push which sent her flying back against the wall. There was a momentary delighted silence. People by now had climbed on chairs to get a better view, and tiers of grinning unshaven faces peered down through the haze. Yvonne was crimson. For a moment she leaned there rigid, as if pinned to the tiles. Then Sam had taken her by the hand and was leading her quickly out of the bar.

Before the heavy doors were shut again they heard the yell which followed them up into the street. "It's safer upstairs, mister!" screamed a woman's voice.

When Yvonne got out onto the pavement she wrenched her hand away from Sam and began to run. She ran like a hare down the dark and ill-smelling street toward the open lamplight of the quays, and here Sam caught her up, leaning against the parapet of the river and drooping her head down and panting.

"Oh my dear darling, didn't I —" Sam began to say; but he was interrupted. Out of the hazy darkness beyond the street lamps a third figure had emerged. It was the thin young man, also at a run. He gripped Sam by the arm.

"No offence, mister," said the young man, "no offence! It was a tribute, a sincere tribute, from one of Ireland's poets — a true poet, mister —" He stood there, still holding onto Sam with one hand, and staring wide-eyed at Yvonne, while the other hand fumbled in his coat pocket.

"That's all right," said Sam. "It wasn't your fault surely. We've just got to go now." He began gently but vigorously to detach the clutching fingers from his arm.

The young man held on tight. "If I could only find me bloody poem," he said, "a sincere tribute, a humble and sincere tribute, to one of the wonders of Nature, a beautiful woman is one of the wonders of Nature, a flower —"

"Yes, yes, all right," said Sam. "We don't mind, we've just got to go now to get our tram."

"— fitting homage," said the young man. "Sweets to the sweet!" He let go abruptly of Sam and struck a graceful attitude. The pose proving too difficult to maintain, he heeled over slowly against the edge of the quay and came into violent contact with one of the metal flower baskets.

"Did I mention flowers?" he cried. "And here they are! Flowers for her, for a gift, for a tribute —" He plunged his fingers into the basket and brought out a handful of geraniums together with a great quantity of earth, all of which fell to the ground in a heap, partly engulfing Yvonne's shoes.

"Come on!" said Sam. But Yvonne had already turned and was walking away very fast, swinging her arms, and shaking her feet as she walked in order to get some of the earth out. Sam followed quickly after her, and the young man followed after Sam, still talking.

"What is her name?" he was crying in an aggrieved tone. "What is her name, who makes rose petals rain from heaven, and with oh such eyes and lips, this was something that I spoke about in a poem —" And as they walked on, the three of them, in Indian file and with quickening pace in the direction of O'Connell Street, the young man plucked the flowers from the baskets and drew their stems through his fingers to gather tight handfuls of petals which he cast high over Sam's head so that they should rain down upon Yvonne.

"Now then, young fellow," said the policeman, who suddenly materialized as the little procession neared O'Connell Bridge. "Let me remind you it's public money is spent on those flowers you are defiling in a way renders you liable for prosecution."

"Nature intended —" the young man began.

"That may well be," said the policeman, "and I intend to have you up for wilful and malicious damages." The two figures converged. Sam and Yvonne drew away.

As they were passing Hannah's bookshop Sam caught up with her. Her face was stony. He began to ask her was she all right.

At first she would say nothing, but turned savagely away over the bridge in the direction of Westmoreland Street. Then she cried in a weary voice, "Oh be silent, I've enough of this, just come to the tram."

Sam raised his hands and then spread them out, opening the palms. For a while he trotted behind her in silence, his plume of black hair bobbing over his eyes. "Yvonne," he said then, "don't go away yet. Let me just make you forget those things. You'll never pardon me if you go away with those things between us."

Yvonne slowed her step and looked round at him sullenly. "It isn't that anything matters," she said, "or that I'm surprised at all. It's that I thought it might be — a specially nice evening. More fool me and that's all!"

Sam's hands clasped themselves in front of him and then spread wide once more. He made her stop now and face him. They were well up the street. "It can be still," he said urgently, "a special evening. Don't spoil it now by being cross. Wait a bit. It's not the last tram yet."

Yvonne hesitated, and let Sam pull her limp arm through his. "But where can we put ourselves at this hour?"

"Never you mind!" said Sam with a sudden confidence. "You come along with me, and if you're a good girl there's something special I've got to show you."

"Something — to show me?" said Yvonne. She let him lead her along in the direction of Grafton Street. As they turned the corner Sam boldly locked his fingers through hers and kneaded her thin hand in the palm of his own. She welcomed him with a very little pressure. So they walked the length of the street linked in a precarious and conscious hold. The dark mass of Stephen's Green was appearing now in front of them and they crossed the road towards it. A few people were gathered still in the golden glow outside the Shelbourne, but on the farther side of the square there was no one. Sam began to draw her along, slinking close beside the railings.

"I'm destroyed walking in these shoes," said Yvonne. "Where is the place you are going to?"

"Here it is," said Sam. He stopped and pointed suddenly to a gap in the railings. "There's a rail out and we can go through inside the garden."

"It's not allowed," said Yvonne, "it's shut to the public now."

"We're not the public, you and me," said Sam. He put his feet boldly through the hole and ducked to the other side. Then with authority he pulled the girl in after him.

She gave a little cry, finding herself in a tangle of damp undergrowth. "It's horrid in here, my stockings are tearing!"

"Give me your hands back," said Sam. He took both her hands and half-lifted her out onto a dark lawn of grass. She took a few steps across its moist spongy surface and then felt the hard grit of the path underneath her feet. They emerged into bright moonlight beside the water. The big moon looked up at them from the lake, clear-cut and almost full, intensely bright.

"Oh dear!" said Yvonne, silenced for a moment by the ghostly radiance. They stood hand in hand looking into the black mirror of the lake, their long moon-shadows stretched out behind them.

Yvonne began to peer nervously about her. "Sam," she said in a whisper, "I don't like this being here, someone'll find us, please let us go back —"

"I won't hurt you," said Sam, whispering too in a caressing exultant tender whisper, "I'll look after you, I'll always look after you. I just wanted to show you something nice."

"Well —?" said Yvonne. She followed him a few steps as he moved, and looked up into his face.

"Here it is," said Sam.

"Where?"

"Here, look —" He reached his hand towards a dark shape.

Yvonne recoiled from him violently. What seemed a monster was there in the darkness. Then she made out that there was a fallen tree lying right across the path beside the lake, its topmost branches just touching the water.

"What is it?" she said with revulsion.

"A fallen tree," said Sam. "I don't know what kind."

Yvonne looked at him. She saw his two eyes

gleam almost cat-like in the darkness in the light of the reflected moon, but they were not looking at her.

"But you were going to show me something."

"Yes, this, the poor tree."

Yvonne was dumb for a moment. Then she came choking into speech. "This was it then you stopped me from the tram for and made me walk a mile for and tear my stockings, just a dirty rotten maggoty old tree!" Her voice rose higher and she hit out wildly with her hand, whipping a flurry of foliage across Sam's round moonlit face.

"But no," said Sam, quite calmly now beside her, "only see it, Yvonne, be quiet for a minute and see it. It's so beautiful, though indeed it's a sad thing for a tree to lie like this, all fresh with its green leaves on the ground, like a flower that's been picked. I know it's a sad thing. But come to me now and we'll be a pair of birds up in the branches." He took her against her will and drew her to him among the rustling leaves which lay in a tall fan across the path.

He kissed the girl very gently on the cheek.

Yvonne got free of his grasp and stumbled back, beating away the leafy twigs from her neck. "Was this all?" she said with violence. "Was this all that you wanted me to see? It's nothing, and I hate it. I hate your beastly tree and its dirt and the worms and beetles falling down inside my dress." She began to cry.

Sam came out of the leaves and stood ruefully beside her, trying to get hold of her hand. "I only wanted to please you," he said. "It's a sad thing to show you, I know, and not very exciting, but I thought it was beautiful, and —"

"I *hate* it," said Yvonne, and began to run away from him across the grass, blubbering as she ran. She was before him at the hole in the railings, and he had to run after her as she hurried along the pavement, trailing a sort of bramble behind her from her skirt.

Now Sam's confidence was all gone. "Yvonne," he called, "don't be holding it against me, Yvonne. I didn't mean —"

"Oh shut up!" said Yvonne.

"Don't be holding it against me."

"Oh stop whingeing!" she said.

The tram for Dun Laoghaire came lurching into sight as Sam still followed after Yvonne, pawing at her arm and asking her to forgive him. Yvonne got onto the tram and without looking back at him climbed the stairs quickly to the top. Sam stood still on the pavement and was left behind, his two hands raised in the air in a gesture of dereliction.

Once upon the tram Yvonne shed no more tears. When she got back to Upper George's Street she fumbled in her bag for the latchkey, which she had not had for long, and let herself into the shop. It was very still in the shop. The familiar smell of wood and old paper made itself quietly known. Behind her the last cars and trams were rumbling by, and in the dark space in front of her was to be heard the heavy breathing of her mother, already sleeping in the inner room. But in the shop it was very silent and all the objects upon the shelves were alert

and quiet like little listening animals. Yvonne stood quite still there for ten minutes, for nearly fifteen minutes. She had never stood still for so long in her whole life. Then she went through into the inner room on tiptoe and began to undress in the dark.

Her mother had taken up the deep centre of the bed as usual. When Yvonne put her knee upon the edge in order to get in, the whole structure groaned and rocked. Her mother woke up.

"It's you, is it?" said Yvonne's mother. "I didn't hear you come in. Well, how did the evening go off? What did you do with yourselves?"

"Oh, nothing special," said Yvonne. She thrust her long legs down under the clothes and reclined stiffly upon the high cold edge of the bed.

"You always say that," said her mother, "but you must have done something."

"Nothing, I say," said Yvonne.

"What did Sam have to show you?"

"Nothing, nothing," she said.

"Don't keep repeating that word at me," said her mother. "Say something else, or has the cat got your tongue?"

"Did you get the Christmas cards with the roses on?" said Yvonne.

"I did not," said her mother, "at tenpence the piece! Have you anything to say at all about your evening, or shall we go to sleep now?"

"Yes," said Yvonne, "I'm going to marry Sam."

"Glory be to God!" said her mother. "So he got you convinced."

"He did not convince me," said Yvonne, "but I'm going to marry him now, I've decided."

"You've decided, have you?" said her mother. "Well, I'm glad of it. And why, may I ask, did your Majesty decide it just to-night?"

"For nothing," said Yvonne, "for nothing, for nothing." She snuggled her head under the sheet and began to slide her hips down toward the centre of the bed.

"You make me tired!" said her mother. "Can you not tell me why at all?"

"No," said Yvonne. "It's a sad thing," she added, "oh, it's a sad thing!" She was silent then and would say no more.

All was quiet at last in the inner room and in the shop. There would be no more trams passing now until the following day. Yvonne Geary buried her face deep in the pillow, so deep that her mother should not be able to hear that she was just starting to cry. The long night was ahead.

# About the Author

Dame Iris Murdoch was born in Dublin in 1919 and died in February 1999. She was one of this century's finest and most influential novelists, whose works include *The Sea, The Sea* (winner of the Booker Prize); *Flight from the Enchanter; The Bell; The Black Prince; The Philosopher's Pupil;* and *The Message to the Planet.* She was also a distinguished philosopher, and in addition wrote plays, a libretto, and a volume of poetry.

# About the Illustrator

Michael McCurdy is a well-known artist. He has illustrated books for David Mamet, Edward Abbey, Harry Crews, Donald Hall, John Muir, Rabindranath Tagore, and X. J. Kennedy, among many others. His wood carvings and drawings appear frequently in national magazines. He lives in Massachusetts.